Weekly Reader Children's Book Club *presents*

Joy Anderson

The Pai-Pai Pig

With illustrations by Jay Yang

Harcourt, Brace & World, Inc., New York

For Jack, who shares islands with me

Library of Congress Catalog Card Number: 67-17150
Printed in the United States of America
Weekly Reader Children's Book Club Edition,
Intermediate Division

If you pet a dragon, be certain to rub his scales in the right direction. —*Taiwanese proverb*

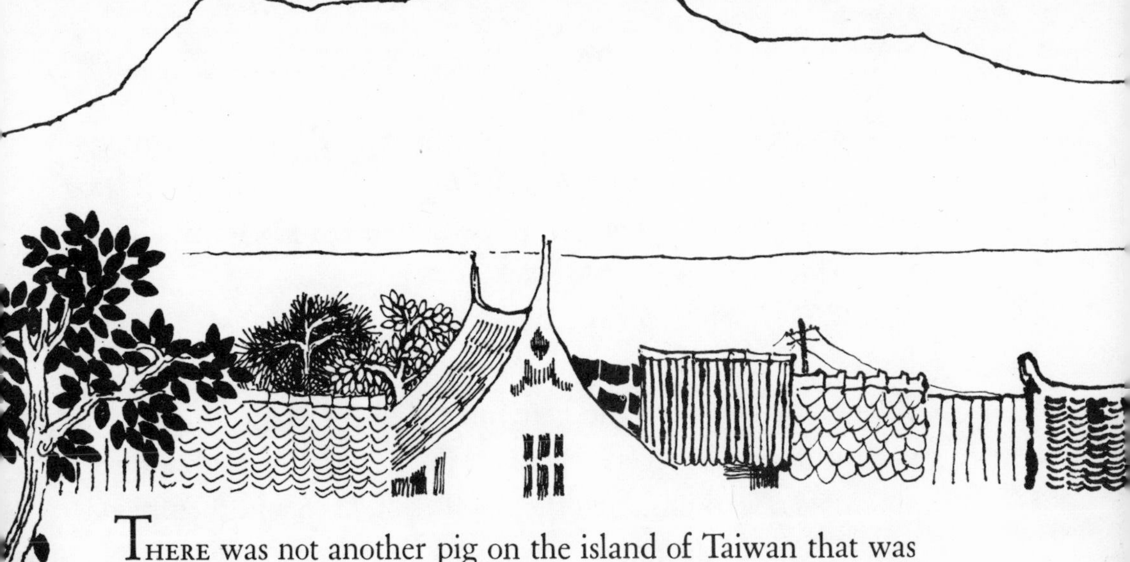

THERE was not another pig on the island of Taiwan that was as beautiful as the pig of Su-Ling Chen. That is what Su-Ling said.

All his friends in the village of Shi-Lin laughed at him.

"Whoever heard of a beautiful pig?" they said. "Pigs are ugly. They have little eyes and big bellies and are good only for eating."

"Not my pig," said Su-Ling. "He is beautiful and I love him. He is the most wonderful pig in all of China and the whole world."

A boy named Yang Yang Lo, who was always a little jealous of Su-Ling, said, "Oh ho, Su-Ling. You have never been even on the other side of Kwan Yin Mountain across the Tamsui River. How do you know your pig is the best pig on the island?"

"Because I think he is," said Su-Ling Chen.

Yang Yang became excited. "Well," he said, "you are wrong. As a matter of fact, *my* pig is the *biggest* in this whole village, and it is going to win the prize at the pai-pai festival next month!"

Su-Ling Chen laughed. "Wait and see," he said. "My pig and I are going to be the happy ones at pai-pai."

Pai-pai! That was the best time of the year in Shi-Lin. It was the day the villagers celebrated the birthday of the Buddhist god Matsu, who protected the families and brought them good luck. What a celebration it was!

There was a parade with fiery-headed dragon dancers, giant clowns on stilts, jugglers, magicians, and lion dancers. There were penny-throw games, Chinese opera, fortunetellers, and fireworks. And at night there was feasting in every house, when friends and relatives came from every part of the island to share the food and fun with the villagers of Shi-Lin. Pai-pai

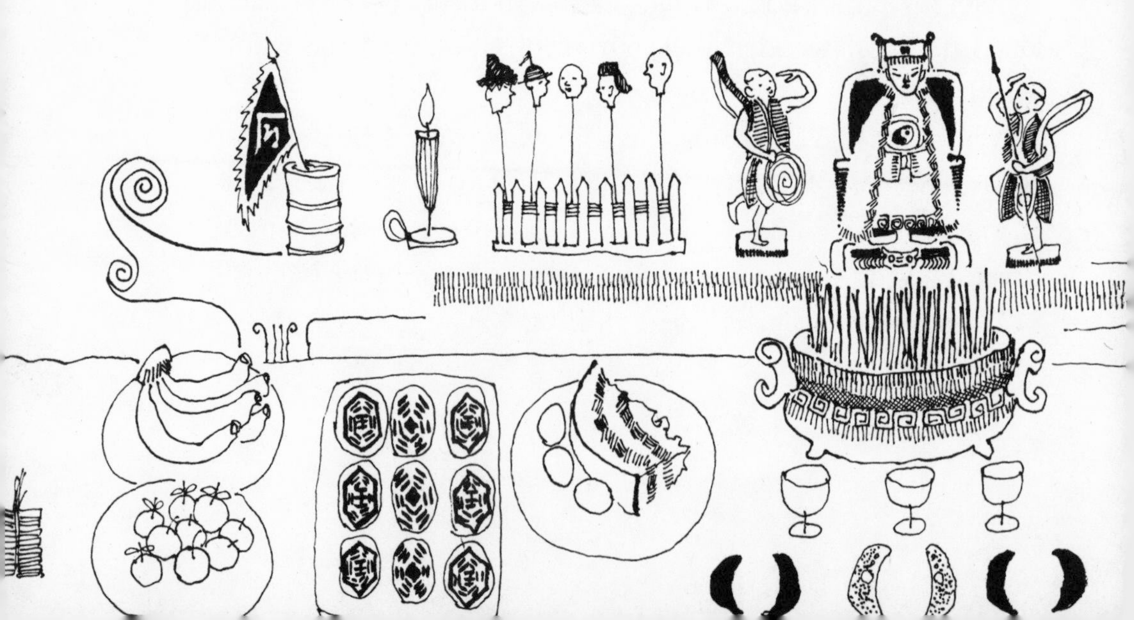

was even better than the Lantern Festival or the dragon boat races.

The most exciting thing about pai-pai was the pig contest! Every village farmer fattened a pig for many months. On the day of pai-pai, all the pigs were weighed. The one that was the heaviest was the winner of the contest! Each farmer hoped to have the fattest pig, for he won a large bag of prize money and a golden banner, gifts from his friends and great honor for his family. It was a fine thing to have the largest pig in Shi-Lin for pai-pai!

This year, Su-Ling and Yang Yang had each been given a pig to raise for pai-pai. Each one thought his was the best. That is why everyone listened when Yang Yang Lo said to Su-Ling Chen, "*My* pig is going to win the prize at pai-pai!"

Yang Yang did not want Su-Ling to win the prize for the largest pig. He tried not to get angry when Su-Ling talked about his wonderful pig, but he could not help it. His face got red, and he shook his fist.

"Let me see your pig," he demanded, "and I will tell you whose is the largest."

"No," said Su-Ling calmly. "No one will see my pig until the morning of the festival, when the pigs are weighed. Then you will see what a marvelous pig I have." He turned away and went down the path to take a swim in the Tamsui River.

Yang Yang looked after him thoughtfully. He didn't know how, but somehow Su-Ling always seemed to get the best of him.

"But *this* time," he thought to himself, "he will not." Yang Yang already imagined his pig with the bag of prize money hanging around his neck. He *must* win the prize!

"I will not waste *my* time swimming in the river," he said. "I must work very hard to fatten my pig," and he rushed home that very moment to feed his pig.

Su-Ling was thinking about his pig, too. But he was not thinking about the prize money. He was thinking about what happened to the pigs after the weighing was finished. After the winner was chosen, all the pigs were killed. That was the part of pai-pai that Su-Ling did not like.

After the pigs were killed, they were mounted on bamboo stands. There, they looked almost alive again, even gay, with rolls of red bread or pineapples in their mouths. There was a great procession of pigs as they were carried to the places of honor surrounding the temple of the god Matsu. Gifts of fish, chickens, ducks, and coins were hung about their necks, and all the villagers admired them, especially the one who had won the grand prize.

If the day was hot, the pigs were protected from the sun by great black umbrellas. Later in the day they were all taken back to the farmhouses, cut up, and cooked for the feast that night. It was truly a day of honor for pigs!

While Yang Yang Lo was imagining his pig with the money hanging about his neck, Su-Ling was thinking of *his* pig stretched out on a bamboo stand with a pineapple or red bread in his mouth. Not a happy, beautiful black pig sleeping in the sun, but a pig soon to be cooked and eaten by a hungry family! *His* pig turned into steaming dishes of pig's feet and thread noodles, and pork and bamboo shoots! Su-Ling's beautiful pig? No. That could not be! If only the pigs did not have to be killed, pai-pai would be perfect. But if the pigs were not killed, there could not be a feast, and how could there be a pai-pai without a feast? Everyone ate pig at pai-pai!

How his friends would laugh if they knew that tears came to Su-Ling's eyes when he thought about his pig being killed and eaten. "Pigs are good only for eating," they would say, but Su-Ling's pig was his *friend*. Su-Ling looked calm, but inside he was turned upside down.

Su-Ling had told Yang Yang Lo that he, Su-Ling, and his pig were going to be the happy ones at pai-pai. Su-Ling knew that could not be true. What could he do?

As he walked through the village by the banks of the Tamsui River, he was full of sad thoughts about his pig. But suddenly an idea started whirling around and around in his head. Su-Ling and his pig *would* be the happy ones at pai-pai! He would make it true! But no one must know what was in Su-Ling's mind. It must be kept secret from everyone!

During the next month, the pigs in the red brick farmhouses were fed cooked vegetables and corn from morning to night. At the house of Yang Yang Lo, there was no resting at all. Poor Yang Yang. He thought only of feeding his pig and keeping him comfortable. What work it was! His pig was immense, but even so, how could he be certain that Su-Ling's pig was not even bigger? Oh, what a worry! Yang Yang never had any time to relax. After each conversation with Su-Ling, he knew that he could not afford to rest a minute!

Su-Ling, on the other hand, was behaving in a most peculiar manner. He seemed to have a great deal of time to play and fly his kite and talk to his friends. Every day he walked alone through the village, taking his time.

What Yang Yang did not know was that Su-Ling's idea was getting bigger in his mind all the time. Not one person in the village of Shi-Lin knew Su-Ling's secret!

Su-Ling talked to his friend Chung, who raised ducks on the banks of the Tamsui River. He watched as Chung shooed the ducks home by beating a rope on the water.

"Chung," he said, "how big do you think my pig is?"

Chung thought for a moment and then said, "Oh, maybe as big as a dragon boat that races on the river."

"Maybe," said Su-Ling, and he walked on.

He saw Yee Ching with baskets of golden tangerines hanging on a pole from her shoulders.

"Yee Ching," said Su-Ling, "do you think my pig is very fierce?"

Yee Ching put her baskets down to rest her back and handed Su-Ling a juicy tangerine.

"Do I think your pig is fierce? He is probably as fierce as the tigers that live in the Mongolian forests."

"You might be right," said Su-Ling.

He walked on through the village, past the fish market with the baskets of tiny dried fish, the fresh shark with sparkling silver fins, the pans of live wriggling eels, and the strings of dried pink cuttlefish hanging in rows.

He passed baskets covering baby ducks. He stopped to look in the druggist's window at the dried toads and the snakes in jars. He went by a great pile of water buffalo horns where a man was making shiny combs from the horns.

He came to a small bamboo stand on wheels, where his friend, Ah Ho, was dipping noodles out of a steaming pot. He pulled a coin from his pocket.

"Ah Ho, please give me a bowl of noodles. I am very hungry. People who work hard picking vegetables for pigs have big appetites."

He sat down at a stool and ate his noodles with wooden chopsticks.

"Ah Ho," he said, "how fat do you think my pig is?"

Ah Ho set chopsticks to dry in the sun. "Your pig might be so fat that he can't stand up to eat his food. Perhaps you have to bring his food on a tray. I have seen pigs that fat."

Su-Ling smiled and said, "Hmmmm. Yes, that is possible, I think." He drank the last of the soup in his bowl and said good-by to Ah Ho.

When he saw the two fierce-looking stone lions at the entrance to the temple, Su-Ling turned and went in. He liked the temple with the incense burning sweetly in the big bronze bowl and the rows of gods with friendly faces. There was Chosu-gang, the soldier, who made life peaceful, and Daido-gang, the doctor, and Gwan-gang, the loyal businessman.

Su-Ling liked to have his fortune told by shaking a stick out of several in a wooden tube and then reading the paper the stick told him to choose. He hoped he had a good fortune today! He was almost afraid to look at his fortune paper. It said: "If you pet a dragon, be certain to rub his scales in the right direction."

His good friend, the monk Hu Shu, with shaved head and long gray gown, was busy cleaning up the gods for pai-pai.

"Hu Shu, do you think my pig will be the largest pig at pai-pai?" Su-Ling asked him.

Hu Shu looked at Su-Ling carefully. His eyes were thoughtful. "I do not know, Su-Ling, if your pig will be the largest. But I know that your pig is as wonderful as you think it is."

Su-Ling burned a stick of incense and placed it in front of Buddha, bowed, and went outside.

That day, Su-Ling met Yang Yang Lo in the marketplace. He was staggering under the weight of two large baskets of vegetables.

"Yang Yang," said Su-Ling. "Are the vegetables for your friend the pig?"

"Yes," said Yang Yang. "They are for my pig. He is so big that he eats many baskets of vegetables each day."

怪談

"Yang Yang, just now as I walked through the village, I have heard it said that my pig is as long as a dragon boat, as fierce as a Mongolian tiger, and so fat that it can't stand up. Have you also heard that?

"Yes, I have heard that, too, and I don't believe it," said Yang Yang. He glowered at Su-Ling. He did not trust him. How could Su-Ling be so confident and calm and carefree, when he, Yang Yang, was tired and cross with the care of his pig? He did not understand it.

Yang Yang thought to himself that if only Su-Ling could see how hard he was working to fatten his pig, he would not then feel so confident. Yang Yang was carrying food to his pig day and night, all the choicest tidbits from his mother's garden, and big bowls of pork and rice from the pots in the kitchen.

The pig had eggs for breakfast and fish for dinner. To stimulate his appetite, Yang Yang fixed delicious dishes of shrimp, mushrooms, and bamboo shoots with delicate seasonings. When Yang Yang had a very fine piece of chicken in his own bowl, he put it aside to give to his pig. There never was a more pampered pig than that!

But that was not all. A pig so petted was not just to be fed and forgotten. He was so fat that he became exhausted from the hot summer days, and Yang Yang took the electric fan from his mother's room and put it in the pig's room so the cool air could refresh him!

He would never allow his little brothers and sisters to go near the pig, for Yang Yang was afraid that if the pig were teased, he might stop eating. Pigs were temperamental!

No one could ask the pig's weight or age in his presence, for he might become angry and lose his appetite! The important thing was that the pig should not miss a meal!

One day Yang Yang found a mosquito on the pig's back. That was terrible! He might get a fever! What a disaster if the pig died before pai-pai and the pig weighing! Yang Yang rushed to the marketplace to buy a mosquito net, which he hung in the pig's room. Every night the pig slept beneath white net like a queen!

What a pig that was! It was a mountain of fat, a pillar of pork! Yang Yang was certain that there had never been a pig in the whole world larger than his. It was not fierce, and it was not too long, but it was so fat that it truly could not stand up. It could not find its own legs. It could not even hold its head up to eat. It just lolled in the shade and waited for Yang Yang to bring it food, and then promptly fell asleep again to wait for the next meal. Since it got no exercise except to open its mouth, it got fatter and fatter!

Yang Yang was nervous and excited. "When the morning of pai-pai comes and the pigs are carried to the marketplace to be weighed, *my* pig will be the biggest. I know it will. I, Yang Yang Lo, will be the one to receive the prize and congratulations and not that lazy dreamer, Su-Ling Chen!"

But secretly he was worried. He had been watching Su-Ling. Why was Su-Ling always in the village talking to his friends? Why was he never working and taking care of *his* pig? Was it because it was already so fat that it could not get any fatter? Was that why he had time every day to fly his kite and swim in the river?

Everywhere he went he talked about his pig, that Su-Ling.

To the pedicab drivers, he said, "Just wait until the day of pai-pai. You will be surprised to see that pig of mine."

To Taiko, who sold purple stalks of sugar cane, he said, "I will take some extra pieces home to my pig as a reward for eating so well."

And to the farmers who came down to the river to cool their water buffalo, he shook his head and said, "I would never have believed that a pig could be bigger than a water buffalo."

To everyone, he talked of nothing but his pig. "It is the lord of pigs," he said proudly.

All the villagers talked together about the pig of Su-Ling Chen. What a monstrous pig it was! It was said to be as long as the freighter that sailed from Taiwan to Hong Kong and as fierce as twenty Mongolian tigers. It was so fat that it had outgrown its own room and now had a special house where a full-time cook prepared food for it both night and day!

Lord Pig! That is what everyone called the pig of Su-Ling Chen, although nobody had ever seen it! Not one person had seen that pig. But the people said to poor Yang Yang Lo, "It is doubtful that anyone has a bigger pig than Su-Ling."

That made Yang Yang work even harder at fattening his pig. He was so worried that he couldn't eat, and while his pig became fatter and fatter, he himself grew thin.

But soon everyone would see this fabulous king of pigs. Pai-pai was almost here!

All the villagers were busy. Mothers were cleaning houses and preparing rooms for guests. They had made rice cakes and Chinese pickle and dried watermelon seeds. The children had helped to dye eggs red to bring good luck. Special dishes were being made in the kitchens: minced pigeon, ducks' tongues, and shark's fin soup.

Carpenters were cutting poles of bamboo to make the stage for the Chinese opera.

The temple for Matsu was ready. Soon bearers would go to nearby villages to bring other gods in palaquins to honor Matsu at pai-pai. Small booths for penny games were lining the street.

This was the most exciting pai-pai of all for Su-Ling and Yang Yang. They liked the fireworks, the opera, the games, and the fortunetellers, but *this* year it was the pig contest they were waiting for!

大殿

At last it was the night before pai-pai! The opera stage was ready. The houses were clean. New clothes were finished. Vendors and clowns had arrived. Gods were in place. Everything was ready. Everyone admired the huge fat pigs in their special rooms next to the kitchens. Who would win the prize for the largest pig?

Yang Yang Lo could not sleep. He was so afraid that something would happen to his pig that he stayed awake the entire night and watched the pig sleep.

The sun burst over the mountains and shone golden on the Tamsui River. When the first light of morning came into Yang Yang's room, his eyes were heavy with weariness. Su-Ling, on the other hand, had slept peacefully all night and did not waken at all until the sun was well up in the sky.

Pai-pai began! The very first thing of the day was the pig contest! How the pigs squealed as they were carried to the marketplace, upside down, with feet tied to bamboo poles! It took four men to carry each fat pig. In the market, each pig was hauled and tugged into a basket and lifted onto the scale.

Everyone came to see. There were old grandmothers hobbling on tiny feet, and babies with wide eyes watching from their mothers' backs. Chung came up from the river. Yee Ching, Ah Ho, and Hu Shu were there. So were the pedicab drivers and Taiko who sold sugar cane.

The pig weighing had started! Who would win the prize for the heaviest pig? There was the first pig on the scale! It weighed 500 pounds! The next one weighed 600! Those were very large pigs! But everyone was waiting for the pigs of Yang Yang Lo and Su-Ling Chen.

Here came Yang Yang! What a bellowing his mountain of pig made! It could surely be heard all the way to Kwan Yin Mountain! Eight men helped to carry that pig! Yang Yang was so proud that he forgot how tired he was and helped to tug and push his pig onto the scale.

The needle on the scale went up and up and up until it reached 1,000 pounds! Yang Yang's pig weighed exactly 1,000 pounds! What a pig! There never had been such a pig in Shi-Lin! It was the largest one anyone had ever seen. Even the people who had been on the mainland of China could not remember a pig so large!

Everyone talked excitedly and whispered that the pig of Su-Ling Chen could surely not be over 1,000 pounds!

But where *was* the pig of Su-Ling Chen? All the pigs had been weighed. Where was Su-Ling? The contest would soon be over. If he did not hurry, he would not be able to enter. He could not be playing with his friends on *this* important morning!

"Here he comes!" someone shouted. "Here comes Su-Ling!"

Everyone stopped looking at the pig of Yang Yang Lo and rushed to see the pig of Su-Ling Chen.

There was Su-Ling. But where was Lord Pig? That pig so big, fat, and fierce that everyone in the village was almost afraid to look at it? Where was this Lord Pig?

Su-Ling walked calmly and slowly toward the marketplace. He was smiling proudly. In back of him, trotting at the end of a rope, was a pig. Not a pig as large as a dragon boat. Not a pig as fierce as a tiger and so fat he could not stand up. Not a pig larger than a water buffalo. This was a smallish, thinnish, tame little black pig! It was a *small, thin* pig!

A gasp came from each person in the crowd. Yang Yang could not believe his eyes.

"Su-Ling!" he shouted. "Where is your pig?

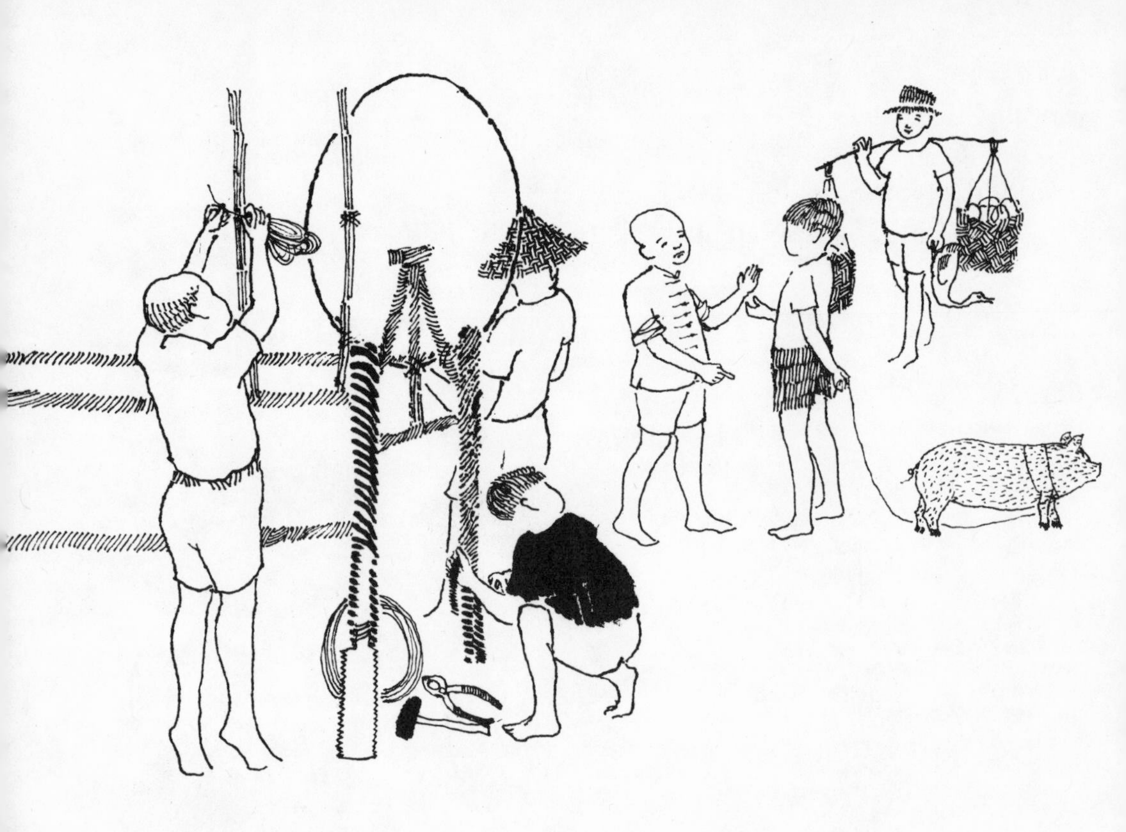

"*This* is my pig," said Su-Ling.

"That cannot be your pig. You said you had the most wonderful pig in all of China!"

"I do."

"But you said you had the fattest pig on the island, the fiercest and largest pig ever seen. This is a skinny little runt of a pig."

"I didn't say I had the largest pig," Su-Ling said. "I said I had the most wonderful and most beautiful pig. Everyone else said all those other things."

Yang Yang shook his head. He was confused. He knew now that he had won the prize for the largest pig, but still he had an uneasy, let-down feeling that Su-Ling Chen had gotten the best of him anyway.

"Why did you do that, Su-Ling? You said you and your pig would be the happy ones at pai-pai. But now you won't win the prize. I will. I don't understand at all," said Yang Yang.

"Well, you see, Yang Yang," said Su-Ling, "my pig is my friend. I do not want to eat him. I would rather have *him* than the prize for the largest pig. But if I hadn't said the things I did, you might not have worked so hard to have the fattest pig! Now you have the prize and I have my pig. While you are eating your pig tonight, I will be *walking* with mine! That is what I want. That is why my pig and I are happy."

All the villagers shook their heads and said to each other that, in his own way, Su-Ling Chen had once more gotten the best of Yang Yang Lo. He was clever, that Su-Ling was, he and his Lord Pig! How he had fooled everybody, putting words in their mouths! And they laughed at themselves the rest of the day each time they saw Su-Ling and that little scrawny black Lord Pig! From that day on the pig was called Lord Pig, although he never got much bigger!

What a pai-pai that was! After the pigs were killed and mounted on the bamboo stands, there was a grand procession as they were carried to the temple of Matsu. Yang Yang's pig had many gifts of honor tied around his neck; chickens, a fish, ducks, and gold coins and seals. Yang Yang got the bag of prize money.

福
頭獎

Su-Ling's pig was so small that it was not even weighed. It walked around on a rope with Su-Ling all day while he played. There was so much to do and see!

The opera began, the actors and actresses dressed in gay costumes and bright make-up. Fireworks exploded. There was a bonfire to burn artificial money in honor of Matsu. Villagers visited Matsu's temple to burn joss sticks and leave offerings of bread, meats, and fruits. In return, they asked Matsu for good luck in the coming year. Many people had their fortunes told. Friends and relatives from other villages admired the pigs, gossiped, and drank rice wine.

The parade! It was the best one Su-Ling had ever seen. There was a band, with cymbals and big brass gongs and bamboo flutes. Lion dancers with red manes danced in and out of the crowd. Small girls rode on seats perched at the tops of tall poles. There were gigantic clowns on stilts with funny and fierce faces that loomed above everyone. Dragon dancers whirled and twisted in front of each shop. The shop owners exploded long strings of firecrackers and gave the dancers money. That chased all evil spirits away for a whole year, they said.

There were penny games of chance and jugglers balancing jugs on their heads as they flipped and turned. Magicians blew clouds of colored smoke out of their sleeves, and clowns leaped through rings of fire!

That night, in the red brick farmhouses, everyone feasted. They ate the shark's fin soup, the minced pigeon, the thread noodles, and the pigs.

"What a delicious pig you raised, Yang Yang," said his friends, eating and smacking their lips. He felt pleased, but not as pleased as he might have had Su-Ling Chen been eating *his* pig, too.

Su-Ling Chen walked home happily with his pig. There was not another pig on the island of Taiwan that was as beautiful as the pig of Su-Ling Chen. That is what Su-Ling said as he stood and watched the sunset with his friends in the village of Shi-Lin that clung to the banks of the green Tamsui River.

And everyone believed him.